In this original trickster tale, the skeleton Señor Calavera arrives unexpectedly at Grandma Beetle's door, requesting that she leave with him right away. "Just a minute," Grandma Beetle tells him. She still has one house to sweep, two pots of tea to boil, three pounds of corn to make into tortillas—and that's just the start! Using both Spanish and English words to tally the preparations, Grandma Beetle cleverly outwits the skeleton and celebrates her birthday with a table full of grandchildren—and one surprise guest.

With its vivacious illustrations and dynamic read-aloud text, this universally funny story is also the perfect introduction to counting in both English and Spanish and a spirited tribute to the rich traditions of Mexican culture.

PRAISE FOR *JUST A MINUTE*

★"Joyful. . . . The rich, lively artwork . . . and spiritual storytelling auger a long, full life for this original folktale."
—*Booklist*, starred review

★"Winking and nodding as she goes, a Latino grandmother will charm readers as she charms Death Himself. . . ."
—*Kirkus Reviews*, starred review

"A delight. . . . This deceptively simple read-aloud treat has as many layers as an onion, and is every bit as savory."
—*School Library Journal*

"A visually striking book, and funny to boot."
—*Publishers Weekly*

A Pura Belpré Award winner
An ALA Notable Book
A Parents' Choice Approved Award winner
A Golden Kite Honor Book
A Notable Book for a Global Society
A Latino Book Award winner
A Tomás Rivera Mexican American Children's Book Award winner

MINUTE

A
Trickster Tale
and
Counting Book

chronicle books·san francisco

By Yuyi Morales

When Grandma Beetle woke at dawn, she heard a knock at the door. And, oh my, waiting outside she found Señor Calavera.

Señor Calavera tipped his hat. What a skinny gentleman! With a pass of his hand he signaled to Grandma Beetle. It was time for her to come along with him.

"Just a minute, Señor Calavera," Grandma Beetle said. "I will go with you right away, I have just **ONE** house to sweep."

Señor Calavera remembered he had extra time today. So he decided to wait.

UNO One swept house, counted Señor Calavera, and he rose from his seat.

"Just a minute, Señor Calavera," Grandma Beetle said. "I will go with you right away, I have just **TWO** pots of tea to boil."

Señor Calavera sighed. Waiting a little longer wouldn't hurt anybody, after all.

DOS Two steaming pots of tea, counted Señor Calavera, and he headed for the door.

"Just a minute, Señor Calavera," Grandma Beetle said. "I will go with you right away, I have just **THREE** pounds of corn to make into tortillas."

Señor Calavera rolled his eyes. He had to be very patient sometimes.

TRES Three stacks of tortillas, counted Señor Calavera, and he put on his hat.

"Just a minute, Señor Calavera," Grandma Beetle said. "I will go with you right away, I have just **FOUR** fruits to slice."

Señor Calavera frowned. This was taking more time than he had expected.

CUATRO Four fruits made into salad, counted Señor Calavera, and he motioned that they should go.

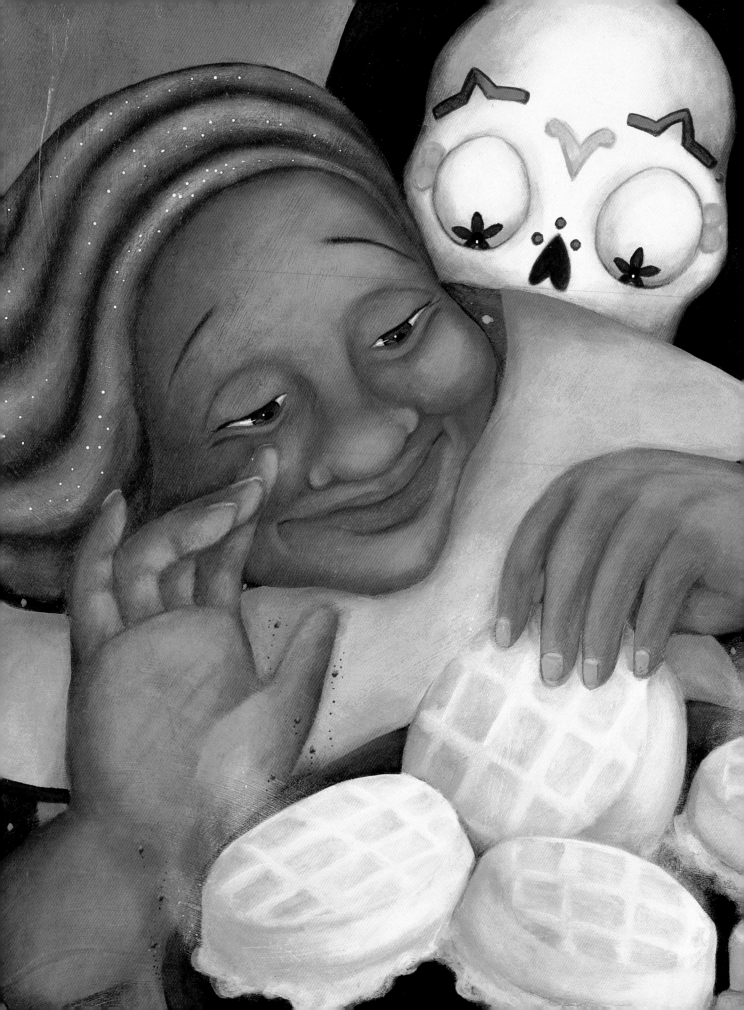

"Just a minute, Señor Galavera," Grandma Beetle said. "I will go with you right away, I have just **FIVE** cheeses to melt."

Señor Galavera tapped his fingers. This was getting out of hand!

CINCO Five melted cheeses, counted Señor Galavera, and he hurried to help Grandma Beetle with her sweater.

"Just a minute, Señor Calavera," Grandma Beetle said. "I will go with you right away, I have just **SIX** pots of food to cook."

Señor Calavera threw up his hands. What else could he do?

SEIS Six pots of delicious food, counted Señor Calavera, and he offered Grandma Beetle his arm.

"Just a minute, Señor Calavera,"
Grandma Beetle said. "I will go
with you right away, I have just
SEVEN piñatas to fill with candy."

Señor Calavera shook his head in disbelief. It was getting late!

SIETE Seven piñatas full of candy, counted Señor Calavera, and he held open the door for Grandma Beetle.

"Just a minute, Señor Calavera," Grandma Beetle said. "I will go with you right away, I have just **EIGHT** platters of food to arrange on the table."

Enough! Señor Calavera could take no more.

OCHO Eight platters of food set on the table, but Señor Calavera had lost count. He was too busy stomping on the floor.

"Oh look, Señor Calavera," Grandma Beetle exclaimed, "here come my grandchildren!"

Señor Calavera took a deep breath. One, two, three, four, five, six, seven, eight, **NINE.**

NUEVE Nine beautiful grandchildren came through the door.

The children sat at the table, everyone at his place.

"Now," Grandma Beetle said, "all my guests are here, and together they make **TEN.**"

But the guests sitting at the table counted only nine.

"Grandma," the children protested, "where's guest number ten?"

"Here he is," she answered. **"DIEZ.**

Number ten, of course, is Señor Calavera."

It was time to celebrate
Grandma Beetle's birthday!

When the birthday cake was
all aflame, Grandma Beetle
blew out the candles with
a gust like a hurricane.

When the party was over Grandma Beetle kissed
her grandchildren one by one.

Then she announced, "I am ready, Señor Calavera."

But, oh my, where was Señor Calavera?
Grandma Beetle found only a note.

Dear Grandma Beetle,
Your birthday party was
a scream! I had fun like
never before. I wouldn't
miss your next birthday
party for anything in
the world. You can count
on that.
    Sincerely Yours,
Señor Calavera

YUYI MORALES is an artist, a Brazilian folk
dancer, a puppet maker, and the former host of a
Spanish-language storytelling radio show for children.
She grew up in Veracruz, Mexico, and now lives with
her husband, son, and cat in Northern California.

To beautiful Eloína, Tia Yola, and my sister Elizabeth.
They dare and I learn. ¡Así de bonita es la vida! –Y. M.

First Chronicle Books LLC paperback edition, published in 2016.
Originally published in hardcover in 2003 by Chronicle Books LLC.

ISBN 978-0-8118-6483-1

The Library of Congress has cataloged the original edition as follows:
Morales, Yuyi.
Just a minute : a trickster tale and counting book / by Yuyi Morales.
p. cm.
Summary: In this version of a traditional tale, Señor Calavera arrives at Grandma Beetle's door,
ready to take her to the next life, but after helping her count, in English and Spanish, as she
makes her birthday preparations, he changes his mind.
ISBN-13: 978-0-8118-3758-3
ISBN-10: 0-8118-3758-0
(1. Folklore–Mexico.) I. Title.
PZ8.1.M7955 Ju 2003
398.2'0972'01–dc21
2002151386

Manufactured in China.

Book design by Sara Gillingham.
Typeset in Barcelona and Posada.
The illustrations in this book were rendered in acrylic and mixed media on paper.

10 9 8 7 6 5 4 3 2 1

Chronicle Books LLC
680 Second Street
San Francisco, California 94107

Chronicle Books—we see things differently. Become part of our community at
www.chroniclekids.com.